This book is dedicated to Carter
Duval Zimmerman

In loving memory of Duval Ryan
Zimmerman, Sr.

Praise for *Carter My Dream, My Reality*

"This book has a powerful message that will penetrate the heart of any reader, both child and adult. With so much happening in our society today, Carter expresses the hearts and minds of children through his fears and through his realities. This book can be used as an educational tool for us all."

   —Blair Underwood, actor

"Becoming a father changed my whole perspective on everything! The book *Carter: My Dream, My Reality* by Tyrell Zimmerman is a wonderful reminder of how much my actions and my decisions as an adult will impact my son's life. Good luck, Carter!"

   —Eric Ebron, NFL

"*Carter: My Dream, My Reality* is a meaningful children's book that will be of interest to adults as well. It's real, relevant, powerful, and engaging. Tyrell Zimmerman has challenged us all to consider how the actions of the adults in our society impact the children in our society. Best wishes, Carter."

   —Ryan Gomes, NBA veteran

"While the world is often a frightening place for children of our cities, this book addresses those fears and provides some powerful life lessons in words of reassurance. What Carter and his mom discuss is an excellent starting point for 'the talk' many parents and their children need to have."

   —Elijah Anderson, Yale University, author of *Code of the Street* and *The Cosmopolitan Canopy*

"No child should have to grow up with the really real fears that Carter has, and yet Carter's reality is the reality of so many kids today. *Carter: My Dream, My Reality* by Mr. Tyrell Zimmerman gives hope to every kid who may fear reality more than fiction. Every adult and child will be touched by this story, and hopefully inspired to be a force for change despite the odds."

-Dr. Jen Welter, first female NFL coach

"*Carter: My Dream, My Reality* by Tyrell Zimmerman is very inspiring. It talks about real life issues. The message in this book can be used as a resource and an educational tool to help us all. Go Carter!"

-Tim Scott, NFL

"*Carter: My Dream, My Reality* has captured a truth I have long held even to this day: that parents, or surrogate parents, can play a crucial role in enabling children to see or experience their reality, and not be limited by it. Carter's mom enabled him to re-imagine his reality as a challenge, so he, with a good education and her support, could navigate successfully; thus becoming an agent of transformation of that reality for others. This is a message I recommend for all of us who are in the position to influence our youth. God bless you, brother Tyrell."

-Bishop Dr. James I. Clark, Jr., presiding apostle of the Church of Our Lord Jesus Christ of the Apostolic Faith, Inc.

"Mr. Tyrell Zimmerman touches on the deep seated mistrust and fears boys and young men of color have of the broader society. I look forward to utilizing this resource to help the youth we serve in our programs."

-Andrew Woods MSW, Hartford Communities That Care

www.mascotbooks.com

Carter: My Dream, My Reality

©2018 Tyrell Zimmerman. All Rights Reserved. No part of this publication may be reproduced, stored in a retrieval system or transmitted in any form by any means electronic, mechanical, or photocopying, recording or otherwise without the permission of the author.

For more information, please contact:
Mascot Books
620 Herndon Parkway, Suite 320
Herndon, VA 20170
info@mascotbooks.com

Library of Congress Control Number: 2017918255

CPSIA Code: PRT1018A
ISBN-13: 978-1-63177-710-3

Printed in the United States

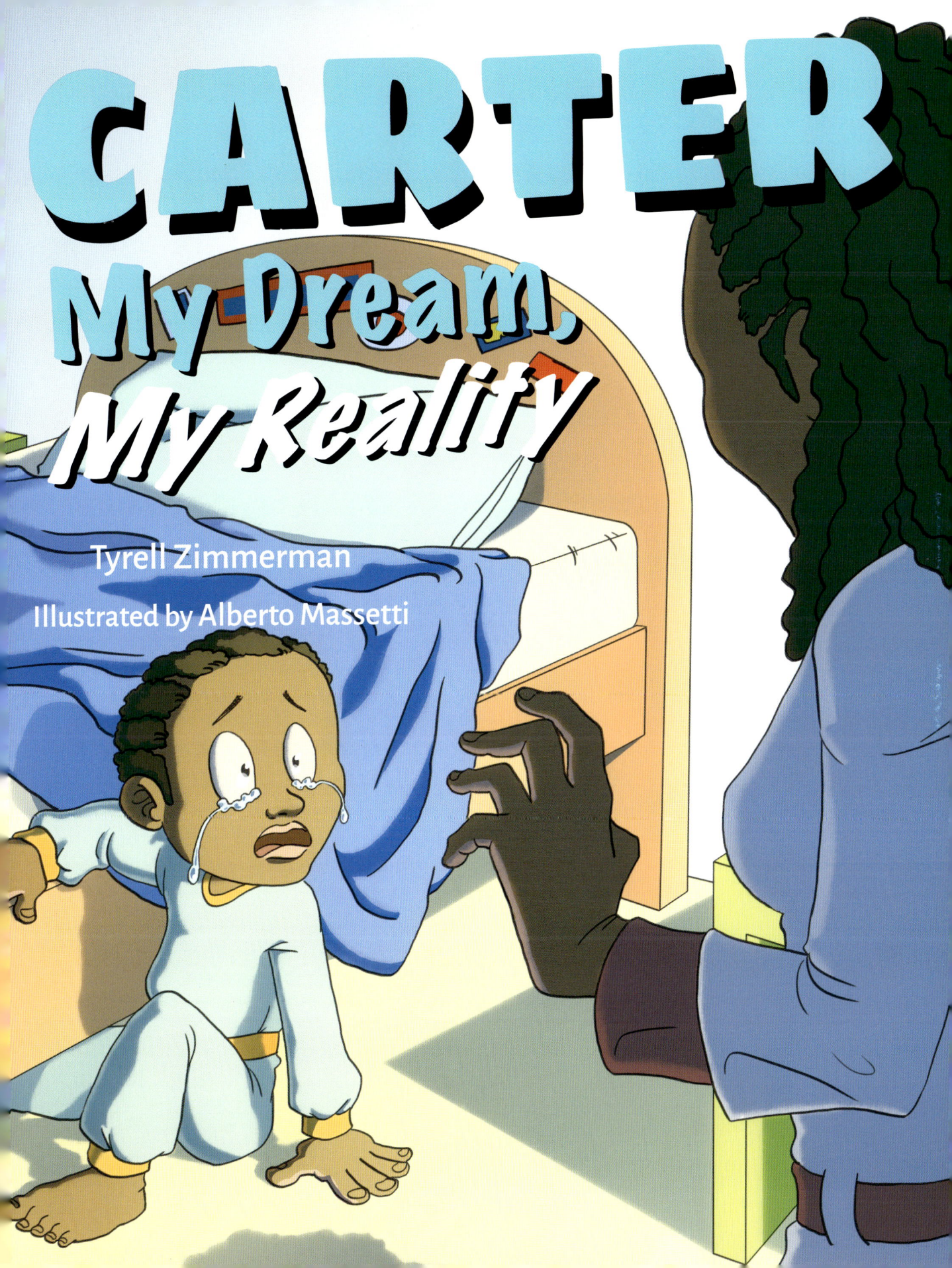

"Good morning, Carter," Carter's mom said loudly. But no one answered. "Carter, where are you?" she said, looking around. "It's time for school."

She looked all around his room, high and low. She even looked in his closet. Carter was nowhere to be found, until finally, she looked under the bed.

"Carter, why are you hiding under your bed and why ain't you getting ready for school?"

Carter poked his head out slowly. "I don't wanna to go to school, Mommy. I don't wanna go!"

"What do you mean, you don't wanna go to school?" Mom asked.

"Because I have dreams of being rich one day so I can take care of you, Mommy. Since Daddy left us, there's no one to take care of us, so I have to take care of us."

"Carter, that is so sweet of you, honey." Mom sighed. "But in order for you to take care of us, you have to go to school and get an education so you can go to college and become a famous football star or basketball star like you've always dreamed about."

"But if I go to school, then that means I have to go outside," Carter mumbled. "I don't wanna go outside, it's scary out there."

"It's not scary out there, don't worry," Mom chuckled. "The big bad wolf or the boogey man won't get you, I promise."

"Yes I do, I do, Mommy," said Carter. "You have to believe me, it's scary out there!"

"How so?" asked Mom. Tears began streaming down Carter's face.

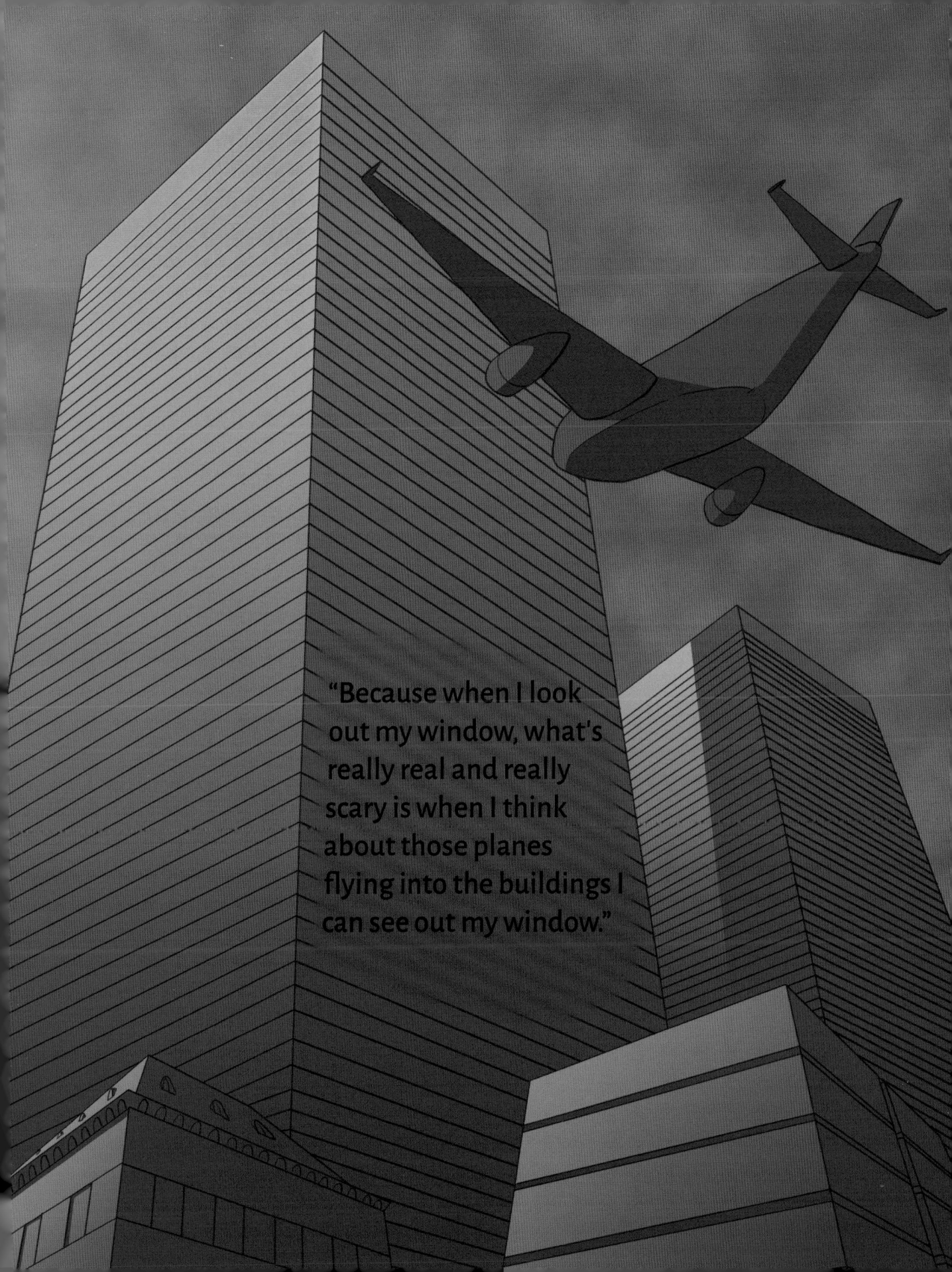

"What's really real and really scary is when I see a bunch of people sleeping outside on the street in the cold with no family and no food, with people walking right past 'em. And when they get thirsty, they get a drink from outside and the water's brown and dirty and makes everyone sick."

"What's really real and really scary is when I hear guys hurting each other for no reason in the middle of the night."

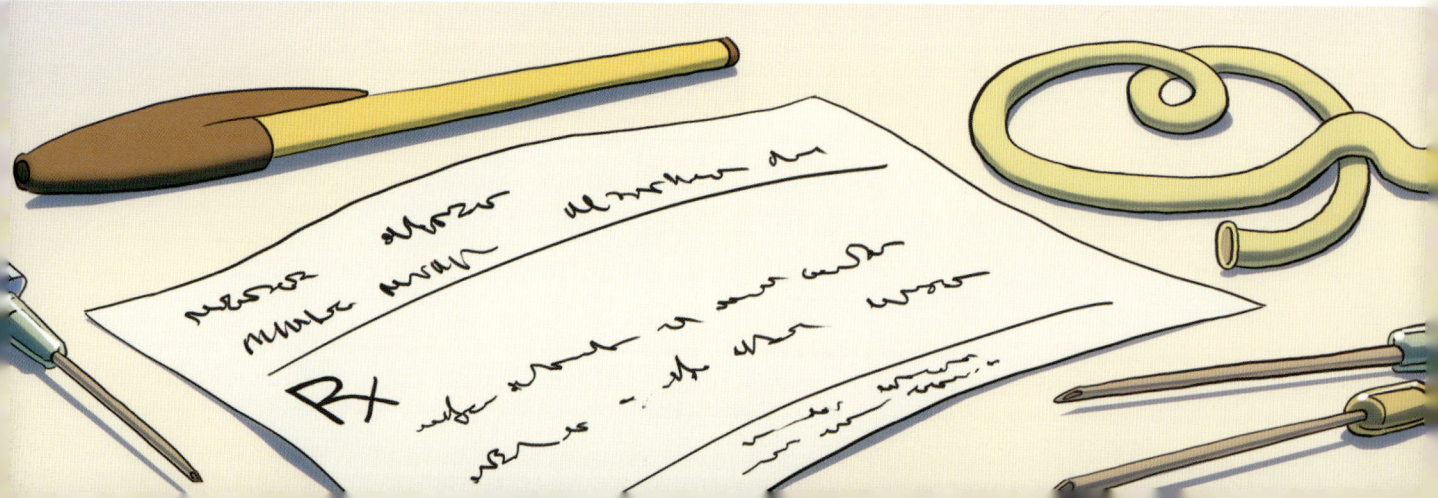

"What's really real and really scary is when people keep going into buildings and schools like mine and hurting other people for nothing. Or when those people keep doing those drugs that make them sick."

"What's really real and really scary is that all the kids I play with at my school don't have a daddy, just like me...Mommy, who's going to protect them and their mommies? Mommy, it's really, really scary out there."

"Carter, you know what's really real and what's really scary?" said Mom in a stern voice. "You holding your hands like a gun. You're right, there are a lot of scary things happening out there in the world today, but one day you'll be a very important and successful man, and all of the young people will listen to you and respect you, like your friends who want to be teachers.

And you better teach them the right way to handle scary things. Show them that they can be whatever they want to be when they grow up. If you do, you'll make a difference in this world. Now go and get dressed and get ready for school!"

Carter stood in silence. "Mommy, you really think I could make a difference in this world one day?"

"Look at me, Carter. You don't have to be scared, you don't have to be afraid. You're not like the people you hear and see out there. You're different. You're special. And most of all, I love you very much. You're my hero," said Mom, smiling broadly.

"I am? I'm your hero?" asked Carter.

"Yes, Carter. You are my hero," said Mom. "And remember, your dream is your reality! One day, if you work hard enough, your dream will become your reality. And then you'll be able to do great things. You will even change the world!"

THE END

A Note from the Author

Dear Carter,

I don't even know where to start. As I am writing this letter, my eyes are filling up with tears. All I can think of is your smile and your big eyes lighting up every time you hear my voice. It reminds me of myself, when I was child. Regardless of what was going on in my life, my dad had a way of capturing my heart!

Losing my dad was very traumatic for me and in many ways left me unprepared for life, feeling alone, and sometimes afraid. But you, Carter, have given me life, courage, and confidence to be the best person that I can possibly be. I had a very difficult and rough childhood, often going without food, clothing, and adequate shelter. Growing up surrounded by poverty, drugs, and violence helped me understand my purpose: to make this world a better place so that one day, you wouldn't have to fear the realities of society and you would be able to confidently pursue your dreams!

Love Always,

Tyrell Zimmerman (Dad)

Praise for *Carter My Dream, My Reality*

"This children's book by Tyrell Zimmerman depicts how children of color feel in everyday society at a young age. I believe this book can be a learning tool for young adolescents."

-Curtis Grant, NFL

"Zimmerman's book provides a developmentally appropriate look at the harsh realities experienced by many youths living in modern urban and toxic environments through the eyes of resilient seven-year-old Carter."

-Jeana R. Bracey, PhD, director of School and Community Initiatives, Child Health and Development Institute

"In the book *Carter: My Dream, My Reality*, there is a message that speaks to us all. It heightens our awareness and brings attention to societal issues that we all have been impacted by. I'm glad that this book can be used as a way for children and adults to have conversations about these things. Good luck, Carter!"

-Syleena Johnson